A Gloucester Trilogy

A Gloucester Trilogy

To: Jim

Nigel Jarrett

All best wishes,
Nigel

12 / 9 / 2019

Templar Fiction

Published in 2019 by Templar Fiction

Fenelon House
Kingsbridge Terrace
58 Dale Road, Matlock, Derbyshire
DE4 3NB

www.templarpoetry.com

ISBN 978-1-911132-44-8

Copyright ©

Nigel Jarrett has asserted his moral right to be identified as the author
of this work in accordance
with the Copyright, Designs and Patents Act 1988

All rights reserved. This book is sold subject to the condition
that it shall not, by way of trade or otherwise, be lent, resold, hired out
or otherwise circulated without the publisher's prior consent, in any form
of binding or cover other than that in which it is published and without
a similar condition including this condition being imposed on
the subsequent purchaser

For permission to reprint or broadcast these stories write to
Templar Media

A CIP catalogue record of this book is available from the British Library

Typeset by Pliny

Acknowledgements

Thanks to Templar for including publication of this pamphlet as part of the inaugural Templar Shorts Award, which I won with the central story here, 'Christ, Ronnie, Christ'.

I'm also grateful for the circumstances which have led to my living for so long in border country between Wales and England, near the southern stretch of the River Wye. On the Gloucestershire side, the Forest of Dean crowds to the bank, like a behemoth come to water.

~

Soft blows the breeze
In Pillowell Wood
As Severn flows to seas
Where the Roman stood
…Anon

The characters and events in these stories are imaginary. They are not intended to bear any resemblance to real happenings or to people living or dead.

A Gloucester Trilogy

~

Three stories

Inspector Rossington's Casebook ~ 1

Christ, Ronnie, Christ ~ 17

Missing ~ 31

Inspector Rossington's Casebook

(Notes for a talk at the Mitcheldean Women's Institute)

Apart from the Dursley pitchfork murders of twenty years ago, I've led a charmed life in the force; if you can call dealing with petty Forest of Dean villains charmed.

I once arrested a farmer who'd driven his tractor on the roads while under the influence; witnesses said it had been an amazing sight. I investigated a sheep theft – a 'major' sheep theft the Western Daily Press called it (well, there were thirty sheep, one black, taken at night in a cattle truck). Then there was the drowned duck business: the result of a plastic duck race for charity on the River Windrush was challenged, and it turned out that some of the ducks had been punctured with a Stanley knife. A fair amount of money had changed hands.

At Dursley that time, in a remote Severnside cottage, a smallholder and his wife were each found pinioned through the neck and chest by a three-pronged pitchfork while tied to upright timbers in their outhouse, a disused cattle shed; they owned land and their deaths were the result of a family acreage dispute involving a schizophrenic nephew returned from Australia. In my occasional talks, I always liken the nephew's return to the appearance, among its annual incoming flights of birds at the nearby Slimbridge Wildfowl Trust, of an interloper, a loner blown off course. I don't pursue the comparison too far, as a single migrant goose is more likely to suffer damage than to inflict it; that's if it survives at all.

That Dursley 'doubler' aside, my career as a police officer was pretty uneventful. Not that my 'nick' wasn't busy. The incident that moved me most was a suicide. A young woman jumped off a cliff above the River Wye, near Symonds Yat. I still think about it, the body falling like a skydiver from a great height, though I wasn't involved in the case. I did answer a call about two stolen cats that turned out to have a gruesome ending. A colleague took over when things became complicated and sinister. I remember the scene-of-crime pictures: there was a lot of blood; human blood.

But there was another incident that still troubles me.

It happened one evening while I was in the office finishing off some paperwork for the courts. Although technically off duty, I was called down by the desk sergeant, who was dealing with a man of my own age, ordinary looking and smartly-dressed but wearing a pair of heavy-duty spectacles that made him look pop-eyed. He had a thin greying moustache, which he persisted in licking at one corner. (I recognised the tic immediately; it was something I was guilty of when I had a full set, until my wife said it made me look retarded, and in any case was unhygienic. That was when you could say 'retarded' and not be slapped on the wrist.)

The man wished to confess to a crime. And not any old crime. The sergeant winked at me, and I wondered if the stranger were known to him as not so much a troublemaker, more a sometimes bothersome 'character'; it wouldn't have been uncommon in those parts. But he must have been trying to alert me to the nature of the confession rather than to the man himself. Perhaps he thought I'd landed a case that would advance my career at last.

It seemed that ten years previously this man had met a woman in a pub, driven her to some secluded spot in the Forest, and had sex with her consent in the back of his car, only for the woman to begin screaming and shouting, and accusing him of rape. The woman had managed to open the car door and stagger away in a state of semi-undress. The man caught up with her, shook her violently and – he had no explanation for what he did next – hit or slapped her, he wasn't sure which; whereupon, she fell backwards and cracked her head on a rock. She was dead, but the man claimed that a mini-second before his hand made contact, the woman groaned and was collapsing anyway. He panicked, placed the body in the car boot and drove to a quiet spot beside the Severn, where he dumped it in the river. Only when he drove back to the scene of the altercation and examined the ground and the rock did he notice that there was no blood, nor was there any in the car boot. He told me she must have suffered a heart attack. No beating heart, no blood. He was a male nurse, working as a temp, and currently between jobs.

We took the man into an interview room, where the sergeant looked after him while I called for assistance on the desk phone. Then I returned, and he began telling his story in more detail. He identified himself, said he had long been estranged from his partner (he gave me her name and last known address and phone number), and supplied a vague description of the woman he claimed to have disposed of. He said he knew of the Severn's high tidal reach, and that when he arrived at the river bank, the tide was on the turn and ebbing fast. I asked him about the weather conditions at the time, hoping to catch him out if he said there'd been a full moon, which we could check, but his recollections on that score were equally hazy: it was dark and, he seemed to recall, damp underfoot. In any case, he claimed to have forgotten the exact day on which the incident occurred, so a weather check wouldn't have been helpful. But he did say it all happened at the end of October, 1989, possibly on a Friday. I thought that was odd: surely you wouldn't forget a date like that. But what did I know? He said he was thirty-seven at the time of the incident he was describing. When I began writing notes, I told him he was born in 1952; he looked surprised (I could only have been a year adrift), as though I knew something that in fact could be easily worked out. Maybe he was startled by what he thought was my quick mental arithmetic.

The sergeant popped his head round the door and asked the man if he'd like a cup of tea. He nodded, and I indicated that I'd like one too.

To be honest, I felt out of my depth. I'd never come across this sort of voluntary confession before. My reaction was to treat the man sympathetically, though if he'd done what he said he'd done, then we were looking at a serious crime. Should we detain him overnight, until my superiors could decide how to proceed? I asked him why he'd decided to confess – and why now. He replied that a decade of guilt had got the better of him. He hoped that, if he were arrested and charged, any court case would give him the opportunity to explain what happened. Maybe the court would treat him leniently if he admitted manslaughter. As it was late, I told him he'd have to be remanded in custody overnight. He didn't seem to mind; he almost expected it. The sergeant sent out for a takeaway and made more tea. Within the hour, my detective-super had arrived, looked at the results of my interview, and went over them with the man again. The assistant chief constable was briefed by phone. It was gone midnight when the man was locked up for the night.

Having been the detective who first took the statements, I went to work the next morning and was provisionally put in charge of investigations. We made some discreet inquiries with his last employer, a nursing home, who confirmed that he'd worked there until he was no longer needed. He gave us the keys to his house so that we could fetch him some clean clothes, toiletries, and other things he'd asked for. I had a swift look around but saw nothing unusual. After more questioning and an early lunch, we took him to the three places that featured in his story: the White Horse Inn, Blakeney; the Wenchford picnic site; and a riverside area near Purton. Meanwhile, at headquarters, a list of UK women officially posted missing since ten years before the incident was being collated, also those immediately after the incident. At least, he could look at photographs and perhaps identify his victim. We knew we might have to go back earlier than that, but the further back we went the more unlikely it was that the woman could be recognised. We were desperate. As I say, the man did give us a description but it was strange, a description of any number of women of what I gathered was someone not much younger than he was; he couldn't think of any distinguishing features, such as a mole or a birthmark. I remember saying to my wife, that if I'd done something like that the woman's appearance would have been etched on my memory. I felt odd when I was telling her, as if I myself might have been capable of such an act – not so much the journey to the river or even what happened in the forest, but the meeting with a strange woman in a pub and going off with her. It was the way my wife looked at me as I was saying this that struck me. We had the man's next-of-kin, a brother he didn't get on with, but held fire on contacting him.

When checking out statements made by suspects and witnesses, we never said why the checks were being made. But in this case we warned that the man's former partner, and anyone she told, would learn of his predicament, one he had placed himself in. Same with the brother. He just shrugged. We showed him the pictures of missing women but he recognised no-one. Some of them were barely adult. As he was leafing through the sheets, I wondered what had happened to those lives, and what my wife would have said could she have seen all those pathetic creatures reduced to lists and data, all that remained of them probably being the photographs, arranged like playing cards in a game of Patience. Records of the few female bodies fished from the Severn since October 1989 were resurrected, but only two remained unidentified, because they were unidentifiable, and the man flinched when he looked at photos of their remains, as anyone would. Often the bodies were found upstream, presumably having travelled up and down twice daily on the tide, like flotsam or, maybe by some combination of weight and volume to do with the laws of flotation, always six feet or so beneath the surface, waving about before rot set in. Others might be discovered well down the Bristol Channel, one at Portishead, another at Lavernock Point. Of course a body dumped in the river might never turn up at all.

    I didn't often take my work home, as the expression goes. I sometimes had the feeling that my wife thought I'd been tainted by the kind of work I did, the people I met, as if criminality were a disease that could be caught and bring you out in a rash. But this case was one to be talked about, because, to tell the truth, at the station we were stumped. After being in custody for two days, the man was told that we could no longer detain him. So as not to give the impression that we thought his story made up or any less serious for being incapable of verifying, we told – no asked – him to keep in touch with us, not that we had any authority to do so. My wife thought it sad that the woman who'd been tipped into the river would never have any comeback. I suppose I did too. Yet without evidence and proof, the whole thing might just as well have not happened. But there were ructions when I suggested that the man should be pitied for not being able to – and I couldn't properly express this – have his guilt, I don't know, recognised. We'd heard his confession but could do nothing about it. Two days my wife and I wandered about the house, avoiding each other's presence, and refusing to have a conversation about anything.

    For a while, the case (it had a number) was a frequent talking-point at the station. We wondered whether the man would call us with some evidence that would allow us to charge him. Now and again, out of boredom, we'd send someone in a car to keep tabs on his address from a distance.

It seemed as though he'd got another job; at least, he regularly went out in the morning and returned in the evening. It was a job at another nursing home. Sometimes, bodies would snag themselves on some impediment in the river or be washed up on a Devon beach - Woolacombe, say. But these, when they were women and from our patch, were too fresh to be our man's victim. Then the case was gradually forgotten, to be raised only when a colleague remembered it. On one such occasion, someone asked about the man's brother, whom he 'didn't get on with'. That immediately made us recall how he'd described his ex-partner as 'estranged' from him. Did that say something about the man and his relationships? This might seem ridiculous, but it's exactly what happens when unsolved cases are revived: the obvious pops up and makes a face at you as though it had been long covered up, when in fact it had been, well, staring at you from the start, as though you'd been slightly dim. Then we never talked about it at all. The sergeant used to call it my 'missed opportunity', my MO. 'Heard anything about your MO?' he'd ask. After a while I ignored him. Later, even he'd stopped referring to the case. I think it might have been his veiled comment on my standard of work, my modus operandi, though I've rarely been called to account for anything – well, nothing much worth comment.

But I have never forgotten it. You could say that it became an obsession, something never far from my thoughts. I would lie awake at night, having finished work late, perhaps after a quick drink with the lads, and having slid into bed beside my sleeping wife. The first thing that intrigued me was why the man hadn't chosen one of those photographs as his victim. Would it have mattered if it hadn't been? His guilt was uppermost, not the fate of the woman he'd got rid of; he must have realised she'd vanished, never to re-appear. Then there was the case itself, totally unique; no-one could remember anything like it. Of course, we used to get attention-seekers, usually halfwits who needed seeing to themselves and who were always claiming to be the suspects we were looking for. You've probably seen them in films, being caught out by the interrogator with a simple trick question. I even visited the places mentioned by the man: had a drink in the pub; went for a walk in the forest and examined closely the bloodless rock on which he said the woman had struck her head; and cycled to the spot where he claimed to have tipped the body into the water. I'd never realised before how, just a couple of miles westwards, the Severn begins to look like the Mississippi as I imagined it: wide, muddy, and apparently slow-moving, though it ebbs and flows at a rate of knots.

    Then the case began to feature regularly in my dreams, as such incidents, often from childhood, tend to do. Though I've rarely been anywhere near an official lambasting, I've always been aware of my shortcomings as a police-officer. I used to think that my slow promotion was due to something about me or my work that my superiors looked upon as only par for the course, even below average. There were always two incidents in my dreams to do with these feelings of inadequacy – I'd be late for a CID exam and run out of time for completing the paper; or I'd spend an eternity driving towards the scene of a crime, only to arrive and find that it had been wrapped up, and a handcuffed suspect was being led away by two other detectives, complete strangers from a neighbouring force, who looked at me with contempt as they walked towards a waiting patrol-car. It's true that I did fail my first CID exam by a couple of marks, but I sailed through the re-sit.

    I've read somewhere that every last one of us hides some guilt away, which will only come to the surface in dreams or on the psychiatrist's couch. And I suppose all married couples go through phases in which one partner, having fielded a hurtful remark, will say something like, 'You need to see someone' or 'There's something very wrong with you'. I've made many such remarks, mainly as a result of stress, in spite of me saying there was nothing remarkable about my career. Maybe that itself has been stressful, and I was unaware of it. None of my superiors ever suggested to me that I might apply for promotion. Sometimes when it was quiet, and having completed a few routine calls, I would drive to May Hill or another high, Gloucestershire landmark and stare into the yonder for no particular reason, except perhaps to remind myself that often there's no-one else around, no-one you can call on, and that you're responsible for everything, every last thing. The 'rippling blue yonder', someone once described it. In high summer it is blue and it does ripple, like a mirage.

My dreams are often confused, though I suppose that, like most people's, it's possible to make sense of them. I began dreaming of that weird 1999 'confession' once it had ceased to be a talking-point. But instead of someone admitting to a murder that could never be proved, the confession in my dream follows a real murder (typical of dreams, the details can never be pinned down), a dead body, an arrest, a denial, a case at crown court, and a dramatic change of plea to guilty, followed by a life sentence. Nowhere is there an explanation of why the defendant decided to confess. There's no doubt that the dream is based on that earlier incident, because sometimes it has features of both: for example, an arrest will be made without a body having been found; or the confession is made, again without a body, but there is an arrest and a court case; or the real incident will be dreamt about as it happened, except that I will be arrested for not having made a case that could stand up before a judge and jury. I often wish that someone else had been at the station that night. Sod's law, my wife said, that I should have been the one. I'm not sure what she meant. It's not that I was never handed difficult cases, or that I had fallen down on the job. Except that, well, something happened during the Dursley pitchfork murders investigation which shouldn't have, even though the case was finally solved.

Ten years after that man confessed to something we could never establish beyond what he told us, I retired. I was fifty-seven, and I'd completed thirty-seven years as a police officer. You could do that then. The pension was good and there were any number of jobs available in private security. I took one, at an Asda store, but it was a dawdle and after two years I retired again, this time through sheer boredom and for good. I'd also got divorced. I felt sorry for my wife: a policeman's wife's lot is not a happy one, a colleague once joked. Many a true word... I only wish she could tell her story. Perhaps she is telling it, and I'm the one who's drifting in and out of her account, unable to have my say. I wonder if she's describing, as asides, things I said and attitudes I adopted, so that people might wonder what I was really like, having been given an impression of the opposite, or a vague inkling that would lead them to get the wrong end of the stick. Anyway, in my retirement I took to exploring the Severn levels, by car and on foot: the Arlingham horseshoe, for instance, with its view of a sunlit Newnham high above the river on the opposite bank.

More than once I found myself in the vicinity of that Dursley smallholding. The place had been abandoned, presumably because of its associations with grisly happenings, though a number of farms down that way were being given up for one reason or another. It was always damp, what with the river mists, and the water table was never far below the surface. The outhouse where the bodies were found had been demolished, but its paved floor was still visible. Oddly, a washing line still stood, and pinned to it or snagged on it was a piece of material, maybe the remains of a garment wind-blown and weathered to a fluttering rag. Squatters, perhaps.

During my years in the force I came across quite a few

bodies. Nothing prepares you for it. Whether it's a tramp still foul-smelling but rotted paper thin in a wood, a teenage motorcyclist lying in the road like a rag doll, or a suicide killed with his own shotgun, the barrel entering the mouth and protruding through what remains of the skull as though no cartridge had been involved, just a violent shove upwards – it was always a shock to see what was once a life become a life no longer. An engineer from the electricity board had found the Dursley bodies. The pair must have phoned him in an emergency because there was no power in the house, no lighting or heat. It was early in the morning, round about dawn, and the back door was swinging on its hinges. He'd called the couple by name but got no answer. A dog started barking in the outhouse and then ran out, not towards the engineer but to begin a circuit of the building, 'sort of aimlessly' the engineer had told us, and then back into the outhouse where it remained silent, apart from a faint whimpering, and out of sight. When I got there, the engineer, told to stay put outside the nearby phone box from where he'd dialled 999, had locked himself in his van. The couple looked odd. Because they were lashed to posts, they were still bolt upright. They'd both been attacked before being tied up and skewered. The man had been impaled through the neck so violently that the pitchfork was still horizontal. His eyes were open and staring, as if pleading for release. The head of the much shorter female was bowed, and it looked as though she were examining her wounds; she'd been spiked through the chest, the heart in fact, but the pitchfork that did for her had not properly penetrated the wooden post and was hanging down, the end of its handle touching the ground and presenting a picture of someone who'd deliberately fallen on its business end. Her eyes were open, too; unlike the husband's – he must have died instantly – her face was contorted. The forensic team thought she'd taken a while to expire. I'd dealt with a handful of murders, but none as shocking as that one. It affected me badly. I tried not to show it.

Well, in short, the Aussie nephew did it, as they say in books, but not before we'd interviewed him and let him go. I say 'we' but although not in charge, it was I who reported that he was not a suspect. Without going into details, I made an error in checking his alibi and he walked away from the station with the usual advice to stay in touch in case we had any further questions. He seemed a nice bloke – gave us lots of information about the couple and how he'd been looking forward to meeting them following the land dispute. I felt sorry for him. I thought he was traumatised. I would have been. Nothing was said about the alibi but I received a lot of surly looks. A better interrogator than I interviewed him and he broke down. A psychiatrist who examined him before we'd got his medical records from Down Under said we were lucky to have caught him close to a further vulnerable 'episode'. Once his alibi had fallen through, he was ours. Why did he stick around? He would have been mad to run off. 'Mad' being the operative word. Although, I've always wondered, but never shared my curiosity, how someone so slight, skinny almost, had the strength to do what he did. If he really did it. These days, detectives go to work every day expecting an appeal to be lodged against some conviction or other they'd helped to bring about.

Not long ago I spoke to someone at headquarters about the 'confession' case. I'd heard they were re-opening old files that had gone cold and were still unsolved. But nothing happened. I could imagine the person I spoke to reporting my call and the other person saying something like, 'Oh, him' or 'Oh, that', and both of them having a joke about it, about me, their sniggering short-lived and not turning to laughter, and they not mentioning my call to anyone else, anyone higher up, and quickly forgetting all about it and about me. He's history, one of them might have said, someone who's done his bit and made no waves.

And it was only then that I thought I might have been privileged, if that's the word, in having been made aware of the perfect crime. What could be more appropriate in confirming perfection than by testing it in the boldest way possible? What could be a greater measure of success than presenting a *fait accompli* to someone – me – who could do nothing about it? Why all the detail if it never happened? And the risk? Well, I don't suppose we can imagine the thrill someone would get from doing such a thing and cheating the authorities. Had our male nurse thought everything out, down to the minutest particular of not identifying his victim from those photos in case the woman he chose at random eventually turned up? (There was a story about such a thing, a family re-united, in the Gloucester Citizen not long ago.) He could have had sex with the woman at a different place, and led us to the wrong one, knowing his explanation for the lack of blood at the scene to be perfectly credible. Then again, my thoughts will sometimes concentrate on him looking at the pictures of missing women, those blurred amateur snapshots we'd borrowed from relatives, and coming across his victim and testing perfection twofold by concealing his response as she looked at him accusingly, or as she did that night at the pub, a woman maybe short on good times taking a chance on what might just turn out to be another one. You see, an undetected crime is not necessarily the perfect crime. Whichever way you look at it, that man's audacity was awesome. Why else would he have come into the station that night? Was he crazy, like the Dursley double-murderer? I'm sticking with the perfect crime explanation. None of us who've been lucky can ever believe our good luck. But I'd love to have seen his face when he left the station for the last time. Was he smiling? Or was his face crumpled with wretchedness? Or was it neutral, unsmiling, and his mind such a mixture of remorse and lunacy that not even he had known why he came to see us that evening, why he had come to see me. Because I've long thought that he knew I was there and I somehow knew he was coming. Silly, isn't it? But there you are. It was my case.

At this time of year, with the sun at midday height, the Arlingham peninsula is at its best. The distance doesn't have to be great to see everything shimmering, as Newnham-on-Severn can be seen all of a wobble across the river on its elevated bank. The water table has dropped to its lowest, and the cows graze without the mist clinging to them or smoking off their backs as if they were on fire. Everything clinging, clasping, seems to have risen, perhaps riding some invisible flame of a thermal, taking the gulls and buzzards with it. Everything is cleansed, free of blemish. On such days, if it's due, I go to Newnham or Minsterworth to watch the Severn Bore surging in against the flow. It was long after I'd thought it was telling me something that I saw it referred to as 'the rolling Nemesis', not an expression you'd hear uttered very often at the Coleford 'nick'. Watching the wave take that long slow bend on its way upriver once every few months, I'm reminded of how nothing bad we do can ever be buried or forgotten, and how it will keep coming back to tap us on the shoulder. That's the case even if we've never done anything to warrant reminding, or if we're so desperate to reveal our wrongdoing, perhaps a lifetime full of little acts of spite and shabbiness, or something much more serious, that at the end of the day we might do anything for redemption. As my wife once said, our view of ourselves is rarely what others see: an ordinary bloke, for example, his relationship turned sour or at an end, meeting in a country pub someone seeking what he is seeking, and everything going wrong, badly wrong. And even if by some twist it became a thing to brag about, the wrongness of it ceasing to be the important part, there'd be no victory over that roller coming inland from the sea, seeking us out and the devil that's in us. It's wider than the river and because of that it roughs up the vegetation below me on the bank. I watch it pass and I stare at the shoulders of the wave settling back and the mallow and the bugloss steadying themselves again after the brief shake-up. And I ride away on my bike, a bit doddery, but like a survivor who cannot believe he's still around.

~

The typewritten notes above were discovered in November 2016 inside a book bought at an Oxfam shop in Shrewsbury. Inspector John Derrick Absalom Rossington was a serving officer in the Gloucestershire Constabulary. He died in 2012 of a colossal heart attack. Approaches to his family have proved inconclusive; in fact, it has resisted further questioning. A constabulary spokesman said there was no record of an interview of the sort described by Inspector Rossington, and refused to confirm that police had received a letter from him written days before his death and addressed to the chief constable, or that its contents had been investigated, particularly in relation to the Red Hart Inn, Blaisdon, Longhope; an undisclosed site in nearby Flaxley Woods; and a riverside area on the southern bank of the Severn, opposite Bullo Pill. No further statement would be made and the matter had been closed. A Mitcheldean WI spokeswoman said Inspector Rossington had been scheduled to give his talk at the opening of its 2012-13 season; members were sorry to hear of his sudden death. Inspector Rossington had not given the Institute secretary the title of his proposed talk, but it was believed to be something to do with the lighter side of his time in the police force.

Christ, Ronnie, Christ

Merrett once saw a woman leap to her death from a high cliff. He was walking in the Forest of Dean, and had reached a crude viewing platform above the river to have lunch. The cliff rose sheer towards him from the water's edge at a point where the flow quickened after its swing around an immemorial horseshoe bend. The platform had been weathered out of the rock, and could be approached by a series of steps off the main path. Above him, the limestone bluff, sprouting growths and soaring vertically, was a fantasy landscape, which seemed to be at its most artful when it began leaning impossibly outwards before the summit.

He noticed the woman perched high and away to his right. She was almost too far for him at first to be certain it was a female, but anyway he thought it odd that the figure he could see was shuffling towards the edge. Then her dress fluttered in the wind. She was carrying no rucksack. That was what made him stop eating and squint. The woman appeared to be alone.

As soon as he realised what might be about to happen – even if innocent, it looked hazardous - she strode smartly like a high-diver, leant forward at an impossible angle and plunged towards the river head first, bouncing off some protruding rocks and falling into the water with a brief, visible commotion, but no sound.

It was a walk Merrett and Nesta had completed many times. He now did it on his own for reasons he didn't fully understand. He called the police as soon as he could get a signal on his phone. There was a report on TV that evening and in the next day's newspaper, and five months later an inquest. He told the coroner what he had already told the police. Although he was the only witness, he didn't tell them – because they never asked and he thought they wouldn't be interested – that there had been a tipping point relating both to the woman's physical precipitation into the void and his own want of reaction at the moment when he might have intervened, if only from afar with a hysterical shout of some kind aimed at attracting the woman's attention, but probably serving only to hasten her end, if she could have heard it at all. Anyway, it had always pained him to have been mute observer that day and not the woman's saviour. That she might have considered salvation to be unwanted was an issue he entertained only much later. But by that time he was becoming seriously forgetful. The woman, who had a history of depression but was believed to have fully recovered, left a suicide note. The coroner's verdict was that she had taken her own life when the balance of her mind was disturbed. She was a young woman – well, thirty-four. Young by our standards.

I'm lucky that Merrett told me so much. When Nesta left him and hitched up with someone else, we became much closer. I believe he walked the old trails, ones he'd covered with her many times, in order to discover if her absence made the experience any different, or if their interest could be sustained without detailed memories of each time she'd been with him. We did a few of them together. I met Nesta only once, at a music festival, so didn't know what caused them to break up. I only had his side of the story and, paradoxically, he listed his own shortcomings while presenting hers as almost non-existent. I'm fairly certain they weren't, and I'm equally sure that he wasn't as bad as he tried to make out. He had no desire for serious attachment with another woman, though there were ones of his own age who thought him desirable. He didn't know my wife, Maureen, who'd been killed in a car crash ten years before while driving somewhere with another man, her lover, when she was supposed to be at a meeting. In the early days, we talked mainly about Nesta and Maureen, the wives we'd lost, in my case permanently, though he now and then phoned Nesta and she him for polite, 'dutiful' conversations. The man unwittingly driving Maureen to her horrible death was a stranger to me. Merrett and I both wandered in vast areas of speculation and the unknowable.

The first time I suspected something might be wrong with Merrett was when he failed to turn up for a lecture we'd decided to attend in Bath. We'd finalised arrangements three days before, and agreed to make our own ways there, he coming by train from his home near Gloucester and I by car from Swindon. We would then have driven back to his place and I would have stayed a few days. Ten minutes before the start of the lecture, when he had still not appeared, I phoned him from my seat in the gardens at Queen Square outside the lecture rooms. I thought it curious that I had to explain to him what he hadn't done; that's the best way I can put it. I remember his first words, because they sounded like a refrain: 'Christ, Ronnie, Christ!' And then – this is a paraphrase – 'I forgot. What am I saying? How could I forget? I've bloody well forgotten about it.' There was silence, the silence of incredulity. I imagined him wondering what might have happened. But I think he knew. Later, I had to force him to admit that he'd been having serious lapses of memory for about a year. Totally forgetting where he'd parked the car in town, for example. Diagnosis would pretty much be a formality. But on that occasion, forgetting he'd planned to go to an event with a friend, me, was a big stride forwards – or backwards.

The lecture we were supposed to have attended together at the Bath Royal Literary and Scientific Institution was called *D. H. Lawrence: Artist In The Background and Other Examples of Literary Effacement,* given by Professor Bronwen Charles, of the University of Trinity St David's, Lampeter. (Perhaps I'm offering supernumerary details to convince myself that my memory is still sound.) It looked intriguing, and its impetus was the discovery a year before of the only known movie footage of Dylan Thomas. The New York film director, Albert Lewin, had shot most of a Hollywood feature called *Pandora and The Flying Dutchman* in Spain, but had come to Pendine Sands, in West Wales, where he'd found the long strand he'd apparently been looking for, and had invited residents to take part as windblown extras. The film starred James Mason and Ava Gardner. There's a scene on the beach involving a car – Pendine was famous as a run for speed trials – but Thomas is not in it; he is, however, in some amateur film taken of the shot, possibly by a member of the crew. It's a fleeting glimpse in the distance of someone identical to the still photograph of him taken with Lewin and a third person on the beach the same day. Well, as one person in the Bath audience stated, it could be Thomas, if the photograph did not show a slightly tubbier figure than the vague background spectre milling around with what one assumed were Lewin's hired amateurs. Maybe Thomas had been included only for his scene to be cut.

Anyway, the episode had sent Professor Charles on a search for instances of literary figures who it was believed had never been recorded, let alone filmed. Her Eureka! moment had arrived, purely by accident, and a Croydon newspaper had beaten her to it. A short film had turned up of a summer carnival procession in the town on Saturday, June 11, 1910, organised by Rechabites and other Temperance groups. As the cameraman, from an elevated position, pans left to right over the heads of the marchers, the forbidding pile of Davidson Road School comes into view, and emerging from the side entrance is a slight, stooped man with a thick moustache and wearing a straw boater. We see the figure turn left into the road and walk away in the same direction as the carnival, as though determinedly heading away from it with a quick, almost effeminate, step. For five seconds, the man's face is seen more or less full on – though in the distance – and for the first two of those in profile as he emerges through the gate, looks right towards the oncoming parade, and skips away from it. It is surely D.H. Lawrence, the image of the man being pursued, as it were, by a procession of militant teetotallers, then seeming faintly risible. Using the latest photo technology, the newspaper had zoomed in on the face and done its best to reconstruct from what were not very sharp images, comparing the result with the much clearer still photographs of Lawrence taken when he started teaching at the school in 1908 and at his wedding party in Kensington on July 13, 1914, with his bride Frieda and their friends,Katherine Mansfield and John Middleton Murry. Someone had even established that Lawrence often went into school on a Saturday to complete work. He was a diligent, if reluctant, pedagogue. It was definitely Lawrence, some expert had said; no doubt. But our Bath dissenter raised similar objections as he had over the Thomas sighting.

The Institution's lectures often turn up the odd contrarian, and so it should. It was a fascinating lecture, Professor Charles having had all the original film transferred to disc. Perhaps their most compelling aspect was the now indelible but limited repeat shot, embodied in her DVD as part of the exegesis, where in other circumstances it might have been played ad infinitum in order to persuade. The professor herself, however, appeared to waver when she ended her talk by commenting, 'What wouldn't we give for two minutes of the voice of David Herbert Lawrence? We have photos, we may have film, we don't have a recording. It's a series of decreasing focus. For Chaucer, of course, we have nothing but the odd engraving or woodcut, even at the time of printing one stage removed from reality.'

I drove straight to Merrett's after the lecture, first having exchanged a few words with Professor Charles. She seemed to like my suggestions of whom one would like to hear on record or see on film. Andrew Marvell was top of my list, followed by Brunel and Walter Scott. One wouldn't want to cast too far back, she said; only to the point where the invention of recording and moving pictures lay unsuspectingly just below the horizon. I mentioned Merrett's absence and the reason for it. I don't know why. She was curious and sympathetic, as if amnesia was something she'd experienced personally. Maybe she too was forgetful, or had a friend or relative who was. She didn't elaborate. Or perhaps she was being genuinely amiable and polite.

When I got to his place, Merrett was watching the end of the ten o' clock news. He looked glum. On a table by his side was an almost empty bottle of wine and a recently poured glass. He held the bottle aloft as an offering, but I declined. I told him I wouldn't mind a coffee. He pointed to the kitchen, inviting me to help myself. We knew our way around each other's places, and we'd done with formality. We began an odd shouting match, he asking me what the lecture had been like, and I explaining things before the kettle began to boil.

This might sound weird, but male friends who have lost their women in circumstances as unfortunate as ours seem jointly depleted. The 'distaff deficits', Merrett called it. We'd stayed together, if that's the right expression, because of our losses. We were friends, but not in the sense of each being independent and choosing to spend time with the other out of mutual interest and similar temperament, or something deeper. In fact, there was a limit to what we could contribute to a friendship before falling out or losing interest, though we never did, not seriously anyway. The Bath lecture was our sort of event: a catalyst for shared enthusiasm and some mild differences of opinion; though I have to say in defence of what might appear to be a conceit in this account that it was Merrett who suggested we attend, perhaps having seen in the description of what the lecture was about some reflection of his own amnesic state, the 'effacement' of familiar things. We maintained a correct distance bordering on stuffiness, and often went for weeks without making contact.

I think we both knew that once our condition had been dealt with and overcome, the relationship depending on it might quickly dissolve. What postponed that eventuality was the lack of equivalence in our deprivation. Prodded by a feeling of injustice, I'd already begun making overtures to other women, not least Professor Charles, whom I seemed to have confronted that evening beyond her zone of authority; whereas Merrett, after the suicide incident especially, succumbed to the weight of an ever-reviving burden of loss. Nesta's absence lurked just beyond him, ready to bear down again, and in that far distant image in Gloucestershire of a woman inching towards her final act, perhaps also battling with some equal and opposite reluctance, he saw his wife on the brink and could banish neither thought nor vision. For it was images we both retained of those final weeks of desperation, in my case supplemented by what I feverishly imagined was taking place. We were both cuckolds, I the savagely dispossessed. We both received condolences.

Despite being literally tired and emotional, he began telling me how serious was his memory loss. 'Like a piledriver dropping with an almighty thump,' was how he described the way it had returned earlier when I phoned to ask where he was. He had a knack of explaining exactly how something like that happened.

'Tell you what,' he said, sliding further into his armchair and in danger of slipping on to the floor, 'I think I'm at that stage we were talking about.'

He didn't elucidate but stared at me, hoping perhaps that I'd forgotten and was having the same problem as himself. Well, I had forgotten – but it wasn't the sort of forgetfulness he was experiencing. For instance, I couldn't remember at that precise moment which pocket my car keys were in, but the realisation wouldn't have worried me.

'What stage? What were we talking about?' I asked.

'When you don't know you've failed to remember.'

'None of us knows we've forgotten something until we're reminded of it, even when it's ourselves who are doing the reminding, realising we've forgotten.'

'Don't you recall? We were talking about not knowing. About not remembering what we're being reminded of.'

'Oh that.'

It was a poor attempt at minimising something I knew was becoming serious.

'Listen,' he said, levering himself upright. 'I lied. Earlier this evening. About forgetting to meet you for the lecture. I don't remember us deciding to go, agreeing to meet. It's gone. Completely. There was no piledriver, no memory returning with a thump. That's what used to happen: piledrivers, thumps. Is this what it's going to be like, the silence of a non-returning memory?'

I hoped it was a rhetorical question, so I contorted my features into a mask of doubt, downturned lips and all, and shook my head timidly towards the negative.

On the mantelpiece was a framed photo of Nesta and another of him and Nesta together. Also other family pictures. He had a son and daughter but no grandchildren – yet. I'd met them once or twice. I hadn't known him that long. Our mutual condition as people left behind through no-one's fault – well, almost no-one in my case – short-circuited the long development of knowledge and trust. I looked at the pictures again, imagining those portrayed as individuals he would some time soon be unable to recognise. I think that's what he really meant: the passage, maybe a fleeting thing, between knowing and not knowing; or maybe something being stutteringly lost, like a standard lamp on a timer come to the end of its illuminating stint and flickering out. He changed the subject.

'Lawrence, eh? Amazing. Did she show the clip, this Professor Charles?'

I gave him a summary of the Professor's lecture, even told him of my brief chat with her.

'Scott?' he exclaimed. 'I wouldn't have chosen Scott. I could imagine what he'd sound like. Moving pictures, though, like the early pioneering movies – that would have been something. Scott, Brunel, or the Duke of Wellington. Imagine it.'

For a man who'd just had to admit that his roll downhill had suddenly accelerated, he sounded thrilled. We decided to look out in the next few weeks for examples of early writers captured on film.

When I left him the next morning he seemed in good spirits and rude health – he always looked pretty fit, what with all that walking. Perhaps he hadn't remembered our conversation, or his lapse earlier the previous night, or even his admission of a lapse. Always interested in ideas and propositions, he wouldn't have surprised me by asking if it were possible to remember what one had forgotten: whether, if you could no longer recognise someone or something, you could be persuaded that you once did and, further, that persistent reminders might lead to the memory's return. But he didn't; and I stopped myself from raising it. Forgetfulness, he once said, just came and went, like memory's subject-matter.

Just over a month later, he phoned to say he'd found something on YouTube: seventeen seconds of James Joyce in Paris. The writer had been filmed, half in close up, chatting slowly to someone out of shot, and spliced on to that was his exit from a house while buttoning a thick black overcoat and being overtaken by a child in fancy-dress, possibly his daughter, Lucia, she who was later to become seriously deranged. It was the day after a message arrived from Professor Charles. I'd emailed her a few days on from the lecture and referred to myself as 'Ronnie Morgan'; she'd signed off with 'Warm wishes, Bronwen'. It was remiss of me, but I emailed her about the Joyce clip before I'd acknowledged Merrett's message, which I did fairly soon, because Bronwen – Professor Charles – replied almost immediately to say she knew of the Joyce footage, but asked whether or not I'd heard the short recording of Joyce reading from Finnegans Wake. I hadn't: I'm not a big Joyce fan. He was just someone, a name, whom reasonably bright seekers-after-knowledge like me and Merrett knew of but had never caught up with. There's too much out there to take in: we stand on the shore, merely paddling in an immense sea and learning from those in the distance who have conquered the waves. I should have realised that the Professor would already have collated as many of these literary snippets as there were to discover. She mentioned a couple: one lasting about ten seconds and, again in Paris, showing Scott Fitzgerald at a writing-table out of doors; and another, lengthier and more complete, of Conan Doyle talking about Sherlock Holmes and then, as if interest in the detective had abandoned him, about his dealings with Spiritualism.

'It was a disaster,' Merrett said, before I'd had chance to tell him about me and Bronwen. He'd met someone while volunteering at a charity shop.

'I was determined not to talk about Nesta but I couldn't help it,' he said. 'It was all she – Moira – wanted to hear from me. She was also – what do they call it? – coming on strong. Perhaps it was part of the way she was taking pity on me, something that in different circumstances I would have hated. Well, that's what I thought, felt. It was as if she were flirting with my shrunken state. It went on for a week or so. More coffees after work, a drink at the pub, and all before she caught the bus home. She refused my offer of a lift. Then, one Friday night, she said she'd have a lift after all. She was a lot of fun and laughed in that way some women have of throwing their heads back and sort of bellowing. It does a man so much good that he gets the wrong idea. When we arrived outside her house she asked me in. And there, sitting watching the TV, was her husband. Nice chap, as it turned out. But, like I say, a disaster.'

I never really knew why Merrett and Nesta had split. Half and half, he told me. I wouldn't have expected him to divulge the whole truth. Nesta would probably have said the same, even if there had been some deep schism due entirely to one or the other. Most people would regard Merrett and me as intelligent, but both of us had lost our wives in one way or the other. There must have been something about us that Nesta and Maureen hadn't liked, because I don't think there was anything about them that either of us, respectively, disliked. Men always want to be in control. The idea of women being in control to the extent of having strong, even breakaway, feelings towards other men is not the same for men as their attitudes towards other women. The guilt, the apprehension, is different. I felt no compunction about having a relationship with Bronwen. In fact, I thought it my right to have one and make sure it worked, which is probably another example of how men's minds operate *vis a vis* women. Although by default, I'd felt freed; whereas Merrett had evidently thought of himself as abandoned. No wonder he'd failed to figure out Moira's intentions, such as they were.

Let me put it another way. My relationship with Bronwen and my attitude towards the fleeting Joyce and the seated talking-head that was Arthur Conan Doyle, the latter streaked vertically with moving stair rods as of someone oblivious to rainfall, were things emerging, whereas Merrett's loss and his failure to revive a love life were conclusive proofs of things gone altogether or in the act of vanishing. For him, I believe, it were as if film had done Scott Fitzgerald, Lawrence, Joyce and Conan Doyle a disservice in not being invented and refined soon enough to bring them into full visual being: its tardiness had resulted in their disappearance.

I prefer not to speak of Merrett's final days. He shouldn't really have been volunteering. He'd been taken into his family's bosom, as the saying goes, and eventually lodged in some kind of nursing home or institution. He wasn't there long enough to make any visit by me useful, though I did go to see him when he was living with his loved-ones. He didn't recognise them, let alone me. The only people he seemed to warm to were the anonymous carers brought in three times a day to see to him. I guessed what that meant.

In the meantime, Bronwen and I had become lovers. I put it like that as an ironic comment on the idea that physical passion at our age can only have a pleasurable, even comic, aspect and can never be the surge that rockets the young into barely controllable regions of ecstasy. We do it because it seems to be no big deal, as they also say, and we know how. It marks no great step forward in our relationship as it would have when we were younger, with the then added undertow of guilt and trepidation. We are both entering the stage of life at which we're defined by what's gone. Even the discovery of each other seemed like no more and no less than we deserved. Neither of us had burdened the other with the details of our pasts and had no plans to consider it an urgent task. For example, I hadn't told Bronwen that Merrett had once seen a young woman leap to her death from a cliff. Maybe I was waiting for the right moment, for it could never be the subject of idle chat. That moment had still yet to arrive when I asked her if she'd like to accompany me on one of Merrett's favourite walks to mark his birthday. She agreed, not knowing that I'd planned to stop for lunch at the spot from which he had witnessed that woman take her young life. Even then, as we sat on the stone bench eating sandwiches and I was looking up at that promontory, I said nothing. It was a beautiful day:

there was a light breeze and I had the balmy feeling of being in motion beside the thoughts of things coming and going in the abstract, not least Merrett's memory of loss and death and Bronwen's loving presence effacing the image of Maureen racing unknowingly to her own violent end.

As my eyes wandered from the river and up the cliff face to the ledge, following the suicide plunge in reverse, I stared at the jutting rock and wondered if anyone would appear there to give me a sense of things coming into being where there was presently nothing at all, an absence as achingly empty as though it were not just lost but had never been. Nothing, no-one, did. At some time, someone would be sitting where we were and another person, a stranger, would venture on to the rock, like Cortez on a peak in Darien (that from a lecture on Keats that Merrett and I had attended), and survey all before them, a landscape as fervid and varied and as dramatic as a life itself, and be recorded by someone else for all time with a camera hidden in a mobile phone. It was at that moment, when I must have been wearing a rueful expression, that Bronwen spoke.

'Smile,' she said, smiling herself and placing a finger on my lips to stretch them gently outwards and upwards. And I did, as if my picture were about to be taken, a picture that would outlive any memory I may treasure of that instant but eventually lose.

We set off again, up the steps that wound off the main path towards the viewing area, with Bronwen in front and me struggling behind. When we reached a level, she was still a little way ahead, walking into a darkened area overhung with a canopy of oak and beech. For a few seconds I was struck with the panic of impending loss as she melted into the dappled greenery and I fought to retain the image I'd just had of her; before she stopped, turned and waited for me to catch up.
'Oh, I forgot to tell you,' she said. 'Someone thinks they've

found some film of Oscar Wilde at the 1900 Paris Exhibition. Well, it could be Wilde. There's only ninety seconds of it and it's claimed a figure in a white suit and bowler hat in the middle ground could be him, part of a moving crush of visitors. I've had someone send it to me.'

As we walked together I imagined her trying to coax this flimsy length of newsreel into something more convincing. A week later she posted it to me on a disc, together with some contemporaneous snapshots of Wilde in Florence and elsewhere and relevant gobbets from a biography. He definitely visited the Exhibition and was fond of wearing a white linen suit at the time. The film is nothing really – just a man, anonymous, out of focus, bereft of all his predicates bar size, shape and dress, walking tantalisingly across the screen before disappearing for good with the rest of that day's shuffling humanity, each of whom was once somebody or other with a claim on someone's attention, if not ours; and all of them coming and going, but mostly going, like a host of shades or perishable thoughts and fading recollections.

Missing

One thing you could never say about *The Talbot Inheritance* was that it failed to cause a rumpus. Not that Emma Brocke was averse to publicity, of whatever sort. She'd written it in all innocence; at interview after interview she'd adduced serendipity as the source of all her fiction, often quoting Graham Greene as saying that *A Burnt Out Case* originated with a chance glimpse, from a boat on an African river, of a white man in a white linen suit entering a hut. Just that. Amazing that I'd never realised who Emma Brocke was.

The Talbot Inheritance began with a sighting, on one of her rambles, of the derelict Georgian-style house near Cannop Ponds. We'd all been aware of it, of course. Through the binoculars she could see its newly boarded-up windows. Some of the boards were rotten or missing. It was a regular occurrence. Since vacated in the late 1970s, the building was barred to trespassers but neither they nor creeping dereliction could be kept out.

The fictional Talbots are eccentric and profligate, and descended from an eighteenth-century sugar planter and slave trader called Valentine Talbot. The novel's gist is that Talbot's heirs are classic epigone, living off what remains of Valentine's wealth but with no reputation in society except as conspicuous spenders and remote and dissipated oddities. Emma had declined to find out more about her re-discovery: the house, called Clearwell Court, and its final occupants, the Hadleigh-Claydons. They were the opposite of the Talbots in almost every respect, and were glad to see the back of Clearwell, which they sold to defray inheritance taxes. Their buyer went bankrupt not long after deathwatch beetle was found in the building's timbers – there was a lot of it – and the place fell into disrepair and ruin. It was now a shell. As freely as the Talbots spent their money, so Richard Hadleigh-Claydon, the family's surviving male heir and a bachelor in his seventies, gave his away. His ancestors had lived impeccable lives. (The Talbots' ironic family motto is *Officium Ante Voluptatem*, a rather literal translation of 'duty before pleasure'.) Richard, living in London, must have read a newspaper piece about Emma and the book – perhaps the one in which she mentioned the ramble and her re-acquaintance among the trees – and been more than a little intrigued. There was an article in the *Telegraph* about writers 'in their place'. Emma, reasonably well-known, had commented on the circumstances which had led to the writing of *The Talbot Inheritance*.

Well, obviously having read the novel, Richard Hadleigh-Claydon sued. One of Emma's surviving Talbots, Sebastian, was Richard to a tee. Not only did the description fit ('tall, handsome, but handicapped by a tripping stammer') there were also a number of other possibly uncomfortable similarities concerning education, career, and associates. Perhaps the most obvious in combination with the others, and the one on which the case against Emma and her publishers rested, was Hadleigh-Claydon's failed investment in a blue-chip company. Sebastian's speculation (not blue chip) is an attempt to recoup gambling losses; the impecunious Hadleigh-Claydon's was to earn money for a trust fund to support a terminally-ill sister, Rebecca. Emma's lawyer decided that her decision to set *The Talbot Inheritance* a short time before the Hadleigh-Claydons left Clearwell; her description of the Talbot's house in the forest as vague and continuously occupied (at the end of the book, the Talbots are throwing a debauched summer party, oblivious of their low standing in society and symbolising the triumph of Swinging Sixties corruption and impropriety); and the success of Sebastian's financial venture compared with the failure of Hadleigh-Claydon's – Rebecca has since died – would be sufficient to convince the court that no-one living could be justified in mistaking one for the other. The book isn't even set specifically in the Forest of Dean, though the description is as good as; it was Emma Brocke's domicile there that raised Richard Hadleigh-Claydon's ire.

And so it turned out. The action failed. Hadleigh-Claydon's only consolation was in the judge's addendum, one of those comments by the judiciary that resort to a dated way of speaking so as to offer opinion as weighty solace outside the law: *'I have to say that were one seeking an example of depravity in fiction,* The Talbot Inheritance *would by no measure be supreme in the history of English literature; equally, as a paradigm of selflessness and the courage required to endure misfortune, the trials of Mr Hadleigh-Claydon and his family might deserve the sympathetic attention of countless others not so encumbered. But that Mr Hadleigh-Claydon should ever be confused with Mr Sebastian Talbot is not to be countenanced by this court. If another judge expressed a different view, however, I would have no hesitation in saying that, in this particular case, one verdict would be very much like another.'* The costs awarded were peppercorn.

Following this brouhaha, there was more. It was confined to downpage items in the quality Press. Law journals took more complex issue with the judge's implication that the libel case could have gone either way depending on who was hearing it. It was even suggested that Emma could have sought redress in the literary Press, based on the suggestion that her innocence or culpability depended on legal 'caprice'. But it all went away.

The biggest stories were in the Gloucestershire papers. Emma was a local, if unassuming, celebrity – a 'Forest writer'. Now and then she gave talks. The albeit guarded reports, with pictures of her, the crumbling Clearwell Court, and the cover of the book with its rococo assemblage of dryads and the cohorts of Pan, ran across two pages, and were padded out by details of the Hadleigh-Claydons and photographs of their family in numerical decline. The judge didn't know, or didn't choose to mention, that Richard was virtually the last of the Hadleigh-Claydons. The family tree had withered but he had long dropped from its uppermost boughs, leaving his depleted chattels behind. He was, as Emma the writer might have put it, fluttering alone in the world.

In her notebooks, Emma – Emma Brocke – tells of seeing a copy of *The Talbot Inheritance* on a charity stall at Ross-on-Wye market cross only hours after finding it again in the town's library. She dithered over the charity copy, picking it up, flicking through it, and looking about her as though the Saturday morning crowds might register a connection, 'a sudden sustained luminosity,' that made them glance her way as book was united with author: writing as self-aggrandisement, almost always lost on the non-writing (and practically non-reading) masses. 'The enlightening sun, burning its way through one of the cross's northern arches, nevertheless promised as much,' she writes.

But she decides to let another buyer choose it, just as she declined to take out the library copy for the sake of recording another loan. Her sister had been a librarian. At one time, librarians had been known to exaggerate the number of borrowings with a little desk-clamped machine, a marker, that they tapped twice or three times whenever a book was taken out. It was done to preserve jobs, to indicate to their dim employers that more use was being made of the library than irregular visits indicated. It was subterfuge, and she was all in favour.

The charity stall copy of *The Talbot Inheritance* was a hardback, tanned at the edges but otherwise appearing unread; remaindered probably, part of a cache spared the ignominy of pulping and doing the rounds of secondhand bookshops and not-for-profit institutions; of which, according to Mark, her husband, she was one. Supportive Mark, so easily persuaded to be unsupportive and now gone with the wind. The one in the library was a paperback version, its front and back curled 'like bacon squirming under a grill' and destined to be withdrawn when worn out, and not replaced.

Sitting in the window of a café opposite the cross, she recalls what was printed on the book's back inside cover below her photogaph: *Emma Brocke was born in Gloucester in 1967 and educated at Ribston Hall High School for Girls, and St. Hugh's College, Oxford, where she read French and German. She worked as a secretary and journalist in Paris and Berlin before the publication in 1994 of her first novel,* Breaking Point, *which won the John Llewellyn Rhys prize and was made into a film directed by Mark Godber, whom she later married.* The Talbot Inheritance *is her fifth novel. She lives in Ruardean, Gloucestershire, with her two cats, Magnus and Clemency.*

The publishers had sent someone to photograph her for that first book. The cameraman, excusing himself ('I hope you don't mind my saying so, but…') as some men did in those days of burgeoning feminism, had described her features as 'striking'. Before his arrival, she'd ruffled her hair – 'raven-haired novelist Emma Brocke' one magazine had called her – and applied Revlon Super-Lustrous Rose lipstick 'with a lascivious extra pressure' that registered in her loins. Mark had dared her to dispense with underwear for the photo shoot, which she did. It was their private joke, until, after too many drinks, he'd made it public at a party. Men, and women more so, thereafter diminished her with their half-smiling glances. It represented for her a walk to the edge, the top of the slide. As it turned out, different head-and-shoulders prints were used for the first three books; only the fourth, *The Pleasure of His Company*, showed her leaning against a fence at Longhope and, unknown to the viewer, knickerless and without a bra. All four pictures were from that first portfolio, some prints of which she'd had framed after the photographer sent them to her unsolicited, which at the time she'd interpreted as a ruse aimed at 'the sort of response that might move fleeting professional acquaintance forward to who knew what – coffee, lunch, dinner, the overnight stay?' Men still did that too. She'd not replied.

She expands on the Saturday morning in Ross. Still in the café, she takes from her handbag a letter. She received lots of correspondence from fans, some brief and necessitating no response, and some lengthy, its involution tempting her – she could not phrase it delicately – into 'the complicity of debate'. That particular letter she'd encouraged. The writer, male but of indeterminate feature and background, had written to her admiringly of *The Pleasure of His Company*, inspired, if that was the right word, by the breakdown of her marriage to Mark. Letters, especially handwritten ones, were almost a novelty. The man's name, Charles Morris, and address – in Somerset – were clearly marked, also his landline phone number, and he'd signed it. It was his second missive: she'd replied to the first, because he'd offered views on male-female relationships and the psychology of mis-matching and marriage deterioration that were interesting, almost applicable to her own case. He was a Classics teacher and a counsellor. She checked name with phone number under BT's residential list and they tallied. She'd replied, making some further points with reference to the main characters in the novel, and didn't necessarily expect a further letter. Two phone calls went unanswered, Anyway, phoning would have been 'too forward', as her mother used to say. In fact there was a month's gap before another letter arrived, with apologies and excuses for the delay. In one paragraph, the correspondent wrote, *I'm sure that love, even when adventurously romantic, can derive sustenance from the retention of a default position. I mean, one can become lost in rapture and still be aware that a way out is possible and at some point desirable. Is it not a reminder of one's inviolable power, first directing intimacy, even to excess, but always knowing when and how to bow out?* In the book, her unempowered heroine (she always called them that), had given herself to her partner without thought for the morrow. One could imagine Emma staring out of the café window, rubbing the re-folded letter against her cheek, and smiling at how it bore no resemblance to the uninvited gift from that photographer; it were almost as if the need for a reply had slipped the letter-writer's mind or that what she'd said in her first reply to him had warranted lengthy consideration. Anyway, she said if he were ever in her part of the world, they should meet. That afternoon, he was on his way to Manchester and would be passing Ross at about 2pm on his way to the M50. He'd given her a mobile number but, like the landline, it went unanswered. No matter. She'd not given him any sort of phone contact: one just didn't. She sent him a text and a postcard in an envelope, with the message, 'Meet you at Pots and Pieces near Ross market cross at 2.30pm. Best wishes, Emma Brocke'.

One imagines Emma having a light lunch at the café and waiting the half hour or so for the letter-writer's arrival. Maybe the prospect of meeting an enthusiast made her recall Mark, a man so unlike her yet with whom she had indulged an ungovernable passion, if *Breaking Point*, not a brilliant movie, was anything to go by – Mark Godber, educated at a comprehensive, a school-leaver at sixteen and a drifter, before he rallied his thoughts and won a place on a course in documentary film-making. From there to directing a feature film of *Breaking Point*, or a version of it for which he wrote the screenplay, was a blurred advancement.

Mark's Wikipedia page is longer than Emma's. Under Early Career, it says he was married to 'Emma Brocke, 1995-1997'. He told *Film Review* that he 'wasn't cut out' for marriage, though he didn't elaborate, except to admit responsibility for the break-up. Emma is slightly more forthcoming in an interview with *Gloucestershire Life* magazine. There's a whole-page colour picture of her sitting cross-legged at her desk but turned towards the camera, the make-up minimal, the waist-length black hair corrupted by cotton strands of disorderly white. She looks serious. She looks as though time, impatient, is waiting for her to sit still long enough for it to re-align her features some more. Her legs, though, are perfectly shaped, seemingly un-aged. *I suppose we were both consumed by our own ambition when we should have been consumed with each other*, she says, not very grammatically and without much originality. But nothing about Ribston Hall High, how it must have been different from Mark's comp, as her time at Oxford surely was, compared with his aimless passage at the University of Life. Ribston Hall, not a place conducive to reservation or criticism, but with high-flyers reaching ever upwards. Ribston Hall pupils, with their crimson blazers and berets, and their crimson gingham summer dresses and white ankle socks with the single crimson hoop. And the prefects, sporting crimson, shield-shaped lapel badges. And Emma Brocke, head prefect, head girl, aflame with talent and purpose. There's no more in her notebook about that day in Ross. But where she ends, I can take over.

I suppose I must have stood in the middle of the market square for about ten minutes, watching Emma Brocke re-read her letter in the café window, order more tea, and gaze up and down the street. When 2.30pm came and went, I saw her take out her mobile. She looked at it for a few seconds before placing it on the table, cupping her chin in her right hand and examining every customer leaving and entering, as if one of them – but which one? – were bringing important news, impatiently awaited. Then she picked up the phone again and tapped in a number. Seconds later, I could feel my own phone rumbling in my pocket. I took it out and cancelled the call without checking the screen, without looking at it even. I stepped down from the Market Hall, looked left and right, and crossed the road to the café. A bell tinkled as I pushed open the door. Emma Brocke peered up at me but I could have been anyone, and she quickly turned away. But I stood there. For an instant she appeared vulnerable. She could feel my presence and turned to face me, to consider me. 'Hello, Emma,' I said.

It hadn't taken me long to find Richard Hadleigh-Claydon after his failed libel suit. I was living in Frome. Every month my brother would send me the weekly Gloucester paper. And one week there she was: *Local Author Wins Court Case: Judge dismisses 'honest' claim for damages.* She appeared triumphant, as well she might. She had also, in a previous life, been Elizabeth Brocklehurst, but I didn't have to read that to know from the picture. With a name like his, Richard Hadleigh-Claydon was easy to trace. He was still living in London, alone as I discovered, and working voluntarily for an overseas charity. Just as I'd waited across the road from Emma Brocke at Ross-on-Wye, so I lingered near the offices of the Commonwealth League Foundation in Islington High Street. I could see Richard now and then – Richard Hadleigh-Claydon – working at a second-floor window. I was sure it was him; his appearance was imprinted on my memory. I'd told him that my father, a Coleford headmaster, Primitive Methodist, and historian, had been writing a book in retirement about old Gloucestershire families but had died before it could be completed, having begun work on the Hadleigh-Claydons of Clearwell Court. It was a lie – about the Hadleigh-Claydons, I mean. He'd agreed to meet me after work. 'Are you t-t-travelling up from Somerset?' he'd asked on the phone. 'No,' I said. 'I have friends in Belsize Park'. Another lie. We went for coffee, oblivious to the pavement blur of commuters. Later, he took me to dinner at a restaurant in Soho, with low lights, seemingly airborne waiters, and muted jazz playing in the background. 'You'll have heard about my brush with the law,' he said. I nodded. I think he was ready to invite me to his apartment near Kings Cross, but I told him my Belsize Park friends would be expecting me. He enjoyed a drink, as my teetotal father would say as an euphemism for a venial lack of moderation. He might also have said it was 'the drink talking' when Richard became tearful while describing his sister's lingering death. He stared at the tablecloth, presumably dredging memories of her, but he might as well have been working out how it had been woven. 'Cynthia Morris – is that a Welsh name?' he asked, glassy-eyed. 'The Hadleigh-Claydons have distant relatives, the Wr-wr-exham Morrises.' I let it be a rhetorical question, and he didn't pursue it. He told me in detail about his unsuccessful bid for damages, in which was incorporated a lot of the information about his family, the sort he assumed I wanted to know. 'Have you c-c-come across Emma Brocke?' he asked. I replied, 'Only when I read about the case in the local paper.' He wrung his hands. 'Ah,' he said, as if my ignorance confirmed the lowly status he wished on her, had it not appeared at the same time to have brought out in his unguarded features a hint of commiseration. I may have exaggerated his stutter. He insisted on seeing that I caught the Tube to Belsize Park. I hopped off early and walked to my hotel.

Lying on the bed in my room and listening to the faint sounds of a city refusing to sleep, I was engulfed by the loneliness that often clothes me when I'm on my own among strangers whose almost furtive impetus is not connected with mine. It rarely lasts long. As a third-former at Ribston Hall High I used to wonder if this lack of contact with others who all seemed to be part of an ever-communicating group meant that I actually did not exist, that my solidity was nothing of the sort but someone else's dream of me. As a teenager in the fifth form, these feelings had still not gone away. But in the gingham bustle, among the swarms in the corridor, I fixed upon a nimbus-girded helpmate. Her name was Elizabeth Brocklehurst. Were we not weaned till then, but sucked on country pleasures, childishly? We soon were. Whenever she came near me, her smile a gift, I almost fainted before her apple-blossom fragrance, her scrubbed-up cleanliness. It was she who, alone with me in the changing-rooms after a netball match and ready to leave, ran her fingers across my fringe and, without comment and encouraged by my unseeing pleasure, kissed me on the cheek. Chapter One. In Chapter Two, out together, she places my hand on the little moist cushion between her legs. I am hot and supine. She obliterates me.

I said 'May I?' and sat down at Emma's table. The café's clientèle seemed superannuated, part decrepit. Not her scene; but perhaps all scenes are hers – mill grist and all that. 'I'm Cynthia Morris,' I said. 'I wrote you a letter; a couple of letters.' She looked first at me then at the other customers to check that this wasn't a practical joke. 'Cynthia Morris,' she echoed. A pause as she worked out the equation. 'Mr Charles Morris from Frome.' She said it like someone bending forwards to read the title beneath an oil painting. I said it, her name: 'Elizabeth. Liz Brocklehurst.' She'd aged more, faster, since that photo in *Gloucestershire Life*. Then she put the bits together: 'I am – was – Liz Brocklehurst. Cynthia, Cynth? My God.' (She'd got the diminutive wrong. I was tempted to jest and say, 'My Goddess, more like'. Well, that's what she once called me.) I knew my time with her was probably about to be cut short, that the high-flyer would fly out of the place, the door bell's tinkle become a jangle. But she surprised me when she calmly opened her bag and took out the letter. Perhaps it was the Emma Brocke in her, the inquisitive author ever seeking material, albeit risky. Before she could say anything more, I explained, though I didn't know where any explanation would lead: 'You see, it was my phone number I gave you, knowing that you might check but find only the name 'C. Morris' in BT's list for Frome. I only pick up Answerphone messages, a habit for people like me, but probably not for you. So you could not speak to me without my checking who the call was from. I made one mistake: saying that I was going to Manchester via the M50. That would be out of my way from Frome, if you'd given it any thought. I *am* off to Manchester, as it happens. But I wanted to call in here to see you.' Which was also not completely true. She was confused, on the verge, I thought, of becoming frightened but not wishing to show it. Even I, remembering the old days of Cyn and Liz - 'Cyn' was our secret – felt momentarily sorry for her. (There appeared a fleeting memory of her kneeling on the bed naked while her parents were out, and pouting at me, her lipstick applied wildly with wanton pleasure. 'Come,' I remember her whispering, as her finger beckoned and her other hand covered her immodesty, 'Come.') Still holding on to the possibility of innocence or soon-to-be-revealed mystery, she waved the letter in front of her. 'You?' she said. I shook my head: 'Richard Hadleigh-Claydon.' I meant it was Richard's idea, but I didn't explain. Maybe it was my imagination, but her face seemed to turn red, and I began to chuckle at the thought that it was not so much red as Ribston Hall crimson, and that the high-flyer was summoning the energy to take off among the café's close-crammed furniture, like some awkward goose. Which she did, presumably without paying her bill. The supping congregation turned to me open-mouthed, tea-cups and morsels held in mid-transfer. With outstretched arms, I feigned bafflement. I ordered a pot of tea and a slice of carrot cake, and took my time over them.

Richard came to Frome often. I think he might have been an older version of me, too – rejected in love that these days mostly dares to speak its name. But at first I didn't ask because we were to be conspirators in a scheme to bring Emma Brocke down, initially a peg or two. Why enlist his help? The idea of enemies united in pursuit of vengeance thrilled me, that's why. We would lie abed, as he used to say, after muddling through. He always apologised, took the blame (he was a downpage performer), which made me seem unfulfilled in the nicest possible way, a woman he could not please because of his own shortcomings, his stammer applying to everything else he did. I acted a lot, pretended. It was an unnecessary rehearsal for five-star performances I knew awaited me elsewhere. One afternoon, we went to Cannop Ponds, then up the track to the remains of Clearwell. As we stood before its façade, I could feel him, much taller, trembling beside me. He had an unfortunate habit of breaking into a sweat at the slightest thing, sometimes at nothing at all, or maybe some internal anguish. He seemed different when he was with me outside London. He mumbled a lot under his breath. On that visit to Clearwell, with crows bursting like shrapnel from the hollow windows, he said something I couldn't make out, picked up a stone, and threw it at the building. He stumbled with the effort. The stone fell short. 'That b-b-book did for me,' he muttered. I heard that. His face, as often, was glossy. He was unforthcoming about how *The Talbot Inheritance* had lowered him in the esteem of its readers. It must have been a personal thing, a sweat-inducer, the private taking of umbrage. For people like him, I guessed, privacy was refuge then redoubt. It was my position too. That night, after more hilarious fumbling, he flopped back and said, 'I should declare my – proclivity.' He'd waited, as stammerers do, to shoot the long word out in one piece. There was silence, before we both detonated with laughter. It must have echoed beyond us, beyond the room, into the night and into the fastnesses of the past. All was jettisoned again: how Liz Brocklehurst, my introduction and guide to shocking *amours*, accused me of molesting her that time we were discovered by Miss Francis in top field; how word got round about me; how I ran away and fell apart; how Liz Brocklehurst, never to speak to me again, was now Emma Brocke, and how they became one in a newspaper article. By the time I'd spilled out all that, I was discreetly weeping. Richard placed his hand on my thigh and squeezed it, no sooner doing so than withdrawing, like someone having crossed a boundary at night and quietly stepping back in the hope that he hadn't been seen.

It was Richard who had suggested the Ross meeting and all the preliminaries. It was I who'd actually written those letters to Emma about *The Pleasure Of His Company,* not bad for a Redbrick graduate (second class honours). Once she'd fled the café, I was satisfied. My satisfaction – at having scared her into thinking that I could do more damage to her thereafter than she'd already done to me – was, I hoped, one that Richard shared. We'd both gone to Ross in his grey Jaguar XKE. He wasn't entirely broke, though the Jag was a noisy classic from the late 1960s. In his sports cap, cravat, and leather-backed driving gloves, he was the epitome of someone who, even considering the other matter, was not my type. While I was meeting Emma, he was visiting St. Mary's Parish Church around the corner, where Ribston first-years, a rivulet of blood, streamed through the main doors each Christmas for the school's carol concert. When I was walking towards the church, I saw Richard approaching. He reminded me of Basil Fawlty, and it was then that I felt that our elaborate assault on Emma Brocke's – Elizabeth Brocklehurst's – pride as punishment for her unacknowledged betrayal had ended successfully. But, still yards away from me, he held up and waved a copy of *The Talbot Inheritance*, perhaps bought from that Market, and shouted, 'She knew. She bloody well knew all along.' His stammer had gone. An elderly shopper, struggling up the slope, stopped and stared at him, at us.

He told me there was something in the book, he couldn't put it into words, that convinced him Emma Brocke knew about the Hadleigh-Claydons, about the interior of Clearwell. We were on our way to Gloucester, as previously arranged. He had to raise his voice above the Jag's roar. 'In the church back there, I re-read the passage in which S-Sebastian is being chased through the house by his f-f-father,' he said. 'Sebastian grabs the marble *Patience on A Monument* at the top of the stairs, and it almost t-topples over.' I wanted more but he fell silent. I assumed there'd been such a statue at Clearwell. 'Might she not have seen it in a book?' I asked, thinking of the Hadleigh-Claydon paragraph my father never wrote. He shook his head. 'But don't you understand?' he said. 'It happened to me. My father, in fun of course, chased me in the same way. There was a *Patience on A Monument* at Clearwell Court.'

Something stopped me asking him how Emma Brocke would have known that, even if it were true, which I now believe it wasn't. Why wouldn't he have spotted it already, at first reading? Why had he bought the damn book again?

Perhaps it was fright, a sudden realisation that I should have gone after Emma Brocke on my own, and for my own satisfaction, and that Richard Hadleigh-Claydon might become a liability. Perhaps I reminded myself that he couldn't bring another libel action, that further discussion of Emma's culpability or innocence was pointless. No – it was the look of triumph on his face, the way he lifted his gloved hands off the steering wheel, re-clamped them, and accelerated away. For once in our escapade, I thought of Emma Brocke. I thought of *The Talbot Inheritance* as possibly the worst of a declining list of titles, the John Llewellyn Rhys prize some long-forgotten milestone to nowhere. I wondered if it were worth my intention to write her a final letter, free of subterfuge and not without an apology, in which I unburdened myself properly and reminded her that though I did Latin and Greek at Keele and she went to Oxbridge I knew that *Labor Ipse Voluptas* would have been a better motto for the Talbots than the one she'd come up with. That night, in a cheap hotel at the city limits, Richard Hadleigh-Claydon and I lay in bed like effigies, saying nothing. He must have interpreted my lack of interest in discussing his theory further as tacit agreement. Every now and then I could feel him trembling, a judder, a spasm. He muttered in his sleep, and sweated some more, beads of dew festooned above his lip. I wanted to go home to Frome. I wanted him to drop me off and drive into the yonder with a belch of smoke, pulling down his cap and waving his gloved hand without looking back. I didn't mention it, but he'd not shaved above his upper lip for three days. Perhaps he was right and Emma Brocke was a fool. Tall and handsome, with a tripping stammer – and a pencil moustache: it might have been a description of Sebastian Talbot. He did go home the next morning, mission accomplished, as he said.

I never wrote that letter, nor did I hear from Richard again, apart from a phone call thanking me for my company on the trip to Ross. I thought that odd: he was my accomplice, not I his. Once or twice on a visit to my brother I've walked to Cannop Ponds and Clearwell, hoping that I wouldn't meet Emma, down from nearby Ruardean. What would I have done? Ignored her, I suppose. But a few weeks on, in my latest weekly digest of news from the Forest, there was another story about 'local author Emma Brocke'. It appeared that her two pedigree cats, Magnus and Clemency, had been missing for a week. 'I'm distraught,' she was reported as saying, 'I've already been burgled once. They never stray far. In fact, they hardly ever go out.' There was a picture of Emma looking at a framed photo of the cats, the perfection of her limbs buried in a pair of unbecoming boots. There was also a smaller picture of a poster tied to a Ruardean lamp-post, itself with photos of the two felines. MISSING, it said. There's something about a pedigree, don't you think; a look of innate superiority, never to be challenged? It brought her into the present again, whereas these days I mostly see her and her modest fame as inhabiting the past, as if she were gone, perhaps for good, like Magnus and Clemency.

I can say now that the only reason I'm able to quote from her notebooks is that two of them, containing the diary entry that led up to our meeting in Ross, have been sent to me anonymously in a plain envelope with a blurred postmark I couldn't read. I've tried to contact Richard but he seems to have vanished. The rest of the later notebook is blank, as though she'd been halted in mid-flow and her further thoughts about that Saturday afternoon were not to be confided. I shudder to think about it. She'd disappeared from my memory for years until I saw her as Emma Brocke in that newspaper feature. Now, she's vanished for a second time. Just like before, I never want to see her again. Speculation would simply weaken the satisfaction of just revenge. I'd given her something to consider and that was all I wanted. For some strange reason, I don't expect to see her mentioned in the papers at all from now on. Ever.

But I do worry slightly; you know, that something awful might be going on.